M000033369

The Witches
of Northboro

by
Anne Schraff

Perfection Learning® Corporation

Logan, Iowa 51546

SPRING HIGH SCHOOL LIBRARY
19428 I-45 NORTH
SPRING TEXAS 77373

$18.95

5/06 Follett

Editor: Pegi Bevins
Cover Illustration: Doug Knutson
Cover Design: Deborah Lea Bell
Michael A. Aspengren

©2000 Perfection Learning® Corporation.
All rights reserved. No part of this book may be
used or reproduced in any manner whatsoever
without written permission from the publisher.

For information, contact
Perfection Learning® Corporation
1000 North Second Avenue, P.O. Box 500
Logan, Iowa 51546-0500.
Tel: 1-800-831-4190 • Fax: 1-712-644-2392
Paperback ISBN 0-7891-5231-2
Cover Craft® ISBN 0-7807-9690-x
Printed in the U.S.A.
3 4 5 6 7 8 PP 08 07 06 05 04 03

SPRING HIGH SCHOOL LIBRARY
19132 I-45 NORTH
SPRING TEXAS 77373

1 "Thomas," Abel Stockton asked his 16-year-old son, "did you visit Aunt Odilia after finishing your chores today? I saw you rushing from the cow yard."

Tom hesitated before answering his father. Not many people in the Massachusetts village of Northboro liked Odilia Prescott. Not even Tom's father, her brother, cared for her much. She was a spirited, independent widow who kept to herself.

"I stopped by for a brief visit, Father," Tom finally admitted. "Aunt Odilia had a clay pot from the Narragansett tribe that she wanted to show me."

Mr. Stockton frowned, causing deep furrows to appear in his brow. "I would rather you did not see my sister as much as you do, Thomas," he said.

"But, Father," Tom said, "I can see no harm in visiting her. She is a good woman. She comes on Meeting Day with the rest of the village to pray."

"That might be," the older man said. "But I oft fear she does so to calm our suspicions concerning darker matters."

"Darker matters?" Tom asked.

Mr. Stockton lowered his voice, although there was no one else in the room. His wife was upstairs with 11-year-old Becky putting the younger children to bed.

"Thomas, when Odilia and I were children, she had odd, worrisome ways," his father said. "Oft times when we quarreled she would make me suffer in ways I could not fathom. She seemed to have the power to make me feel pinpricks from across the room. It was . . . disturbing."

Tom stared at his father. What was he saying? A year ago in 1659, four women from a nearby village had been arrested and condemned as witches. According to witnesses, the women had displayed the same type of behavior his father was describing, casting spells on people and making them feel as if they were being bitten or pinched.

"Surely you are not suggesting that Aunt Odilia has dark powers?" Tom cried incredulously.

"Do not mock me, Thomas," Mr.

Stockton scolded. "I only know that throughout Massachusetts there are rumors of witches doing dastardly things. If ever Odilia should fall under suspicion, I want none of my family found guilty of associating with her."

Guilty of associating with her? Tom wondered. How could he *not* associate with her? Tom felt closer to his aunt than to his own parents. He considered her to be a kindred spirit, one who was of a similar nature to him. Like Odilia, Tom was inquisitive and a dreamer. And like Odilia, Tom had thick, dark hair and bright green eyes.

Aunt Odilia's late husband had been a seafaring man. Tom loved to hear her tales of wild storms and strange foreign isles. Uncle Nehemiah had died in a frightful Atlantic gale years ago. Now Aunt Odilia lived in a house weathered to silver with only chickens and three pigs for company. And Tom went to visit her every chance he got.

Just then Tom's mother came down the stairs. "Well," she said, "the little ones are asleep. But Becky is still restless. What an imaginative child she is! Every little creak in the beams makes her suspect some amazing animal has climbed onto the roof."

Tom noticed distress on his father's face at the comment. He wondered what was going through the older man's mind. He didn't have long to wait to find out.

"I pray my sister's contrary spirit has not passed to our Becky," Mr. Stockton worried.

His wife laughed. "Oh, Abel, Becky is simply a lively girl. What sin is there in that? She is the one who brightens the house. She greets every new day with relish, as if it were a gift from God."

She's right, Tom thought. Six-year-old Ann had a quiet, almost cautious manner about her. Elizabeth, at eight, was a shy, awkward girl. And serious little Samuel rarely cried. But Becky was as wild as a young filly let loose to romp in the meadows. She had spirit, true. But not a contrary spirit, Tom was sure.

He didn't think his aunt was contrary either. And he had no intention of ceasing his visits. They were too enjoyable. The humdrum life of the farm did not compare to Aunt Odilia's accounts of Uncle Nehemiah's battles with monster whales. Or how his ship was becalmed on the open sea for 20 days, and he and his crew almost died of hunger and thirst until a wind appeared from nowhere to save them.

Tom often dreamed of going to sea himself. He agreed with Aunt Odilia's description of farm life. "Nothing but endless fields and hard, hot work with nary a glimpse of freedom," she'd often say. Aunt Odilia was for Tom a window through which he could see a wider, more exciting world. And although he hadn't told his parents, Tom hoped to see that world for himself one day.

* * *

Early Saturday afternoon, some of the young people of Northboro went on a hayride. For a time, Tom was able to forget his father's ramblings about witches. Helping him to forget was the daughter of a family that had just moved to Northboro. Perched prettily atop a bale of hay, tall, fair-haired Martha Burnside smiled at Tom from beneath her dainty blue bonnet. Tom smiled back eagerly. There were other pretty girls in Northboro. But Martha was the one who had really caught his fancy.

"How does your father make his living?" Tom asked Martha as the wagon bounced along the rutted road.

"He's a chandler," Martha replied. "He has taken over the business of Mr. Fezwelder. Mr. Fezwelder said he was getting too old to stoop over, making candles all day."

"Yes," Tom said. "Josiah Fezwelder has been ailing with rheumatic pain for years. I'm sure he needs the rest."

As the hay wagon reached the outskirts of Northboro, Tom and Martha talked continuously. Tom felt very much at ease with the girl. When the young people began singing, Tom and Martha joined in. Their voices rose heartily above all the others. The two looked at each other and smiled, both recognizing how well-suited they were to each other.

Suddenly the happy group was stopped by a disquieting sight.

"Look! Over there!" Peter Garson yelled as they passed Widow Manwell's old farmhouse. Peter was a friend of Tom's.

Everyone looked as the driver brought the team of horses to a halt. There at the gate stood a girl of about 11. As the group watched, the girl dashed herself against the rotting fence post that held the gate. Then she rolled in the dirt and screamed lustily.

"Oh, dear," Martha said, "we must help that poor child."

Tom recognized the girl. It was Agatha Palmer, the daughter of the village blacksmith. Agatha was an only child, a rare thing in Northboro where most families had many children. She spent most of her time with her dour mother and father because she had few friends. Agatha had a selfish personality and never played well with girls her own age. In fact, she was known for the terrible tantrums she threw whenever she didn't get her way.

Tom and Peter jumped off the wagon.

They approached Agatha, who continued to thrash about and howl.

"Aggie," Tom shouted, "what's the matter?"

"Calm yourself, Aggie," Peter said.

"Were you bitten by a mad dog?" Tom asked.

"No, no," Agatha sobbed, allowing Tom to pull her to her feet. "No dog has done this to me. *She* did it. *She* is tormenting me! *She* is pulling my hair and pouring scalding liquid down my throat!"

Tom and Peter looked at each other. Both boys shook their heads in puzzlement.

"Aggie, who is doing these things to you?" Tom asked.

"The witch," Agatha cried, twitching violently. "Can't you see the witch?"

Tom glanced around the quiet meadow. So did the others. Nobody saw anything.

"I don't see any witch," Tom said.

"Nor do I," said Peter.

"Up there! She's perched in that tree. You must see her!" Agatha shrieked.

"I see an old blackbird," Peter said, scratching his head.

"That's her!" Agatha insisted. "She can

change into a bird, or a cat, or a mouse!" Then she held up a bleeding forearm. "Look how she bit me!"

The two boys looked closely at the girl's arm. There were teeth marks on it all right.

"You sure you didn't get so excited that you bit yourself, Aggie?" Tom asked, looking the young girl over. Her hair was a tangled mess, and her dress was torn. "You seem to be pretty worked up."

Agatha glared at Tom. Then she picked up her skirts and ran off without another word.

Tom might have laughed the whole incident away as one of Agatha Palmer's tantrums. But he remembered his conversation with his father about witches, and he felt a bit uneasy. Would the frightening madness of a witchcraft scare strike in Northboro? he wondered.

"She's a strange one," Peter said, shaking his head. "Her whole family is strange. I have never seen any one of them smile."

"Where would a girl that age get such notions?" Tom wondered aloud.

Martha spoke up. "In the village I just

came from, there is much fear of witches. Two milk cows died from no cause, and everyone was sure a witch had cursed them."

"Well, I think Dr. Brewster needs to look at Aggie," Tom said, trying to steer the conversation away from the topic of witches. "She must have a fever."

Tom and Peter reboarded the hay wagon, and it continued on its way.

"Will you farm as your father does, Tom?" Martha asked after a few minutes.

"I have thought of going to sea," Tom said. "Uncle Nehemiah oft said that a boy becomes a man when he goes to sea. But Father has offered me the back half of our farm to raise a house on when I marry. It would please him if I did that."

"But would it please you?" Martha asked.

"I'm not sure," Tom replied. Settling down on a farm had never appealed to him much. But now, looking at Martha, he changed his mind a bit. A seafaring man was not a good prospect for a husband, at least that's what Aunt Odilia had told him. He remembered her once telling him, "It was as if I became a widow long before he dropped to the bottom of the sea. I scarce saw him for a week or a month before he was gone again. Each time he returned, I counted it as a miracle, knowing in my heart that with each farewell, I might never see him again."

"Tom, have you ever seen a witch?" Martha asked.

"I have never seen anything of the sort," Tom said firmly.

"You have never seen something strange that you could not explain, some spectral sight flitting before you?" Martha asked.

Tom turned to look at the girl, at her clear blue eyes and her lovely oval face. "Well, have *you*, Martha? Have you seen a witch?" he asked.

"I don't know," Martha replied. "In the village where we lived, there was an old woman who had a crooked leg. She walked with great difficulty. Oft times the boys of the village would mock her, limping after her and laughing at her deformity. It was said that one day she put a curse on them."

"What kind of curse?" Tom asked, not believing Martha's story.

"She made them itch," Martha explained. "That's what the boys said. They itched all summer as if bitten by mosquitoes. Nothing gave them relief. One of them went to the old woman and pleaded with her to lift the curse, and so it was. That boy was cured of his torment. But the other boys suffered all summer until the first snowfall."

"They must have tumbled into some noxious weed that caused their affliction," Tom said. "Imagination tricks us, Martha. My little sister, Becky, is sure she sees an old man's face in the moon. No, Martha, I doubt that we shall ever see a witch in Northboro."

"Perhaps you're right," Martha replied. "But Agatha Palmer believes she has already seen one."

2 A fierce storm blew up early that evening. It began with a single gray line across the sky but soon built to masses of clouds and darkness.

Becky sat by the window, looking outside. "See how the birds flee," she observed. "They know a big storm is coming. Do you think there will be thunder and lightning, Mother? Oh, I do hope so."

"More than likely," Mrs. Stockton replied. "I just hope that the wind does not wreak havoc with the animal sheds. Do you remember last year when the poor chickens were almost blown away?"

Her husband nodded gravely. "These storms are much to be feared."

Becky looked annoyed. "Father, Mother, why must you be unhappy about something as wonderful as a storm?" she asked. Her bright blue eyes danced with excitement. "It is such a beautiful sight to see the clouds go by like sailing ships bobbing on a great dark sea!"

"What a strange notion to call something as dark and destructive as a storm beautiful, child," Mr. Stockton said.

He looked at his daughter with fresh concern.

Tom noticed his father's worried look, but he smiled at his younger sister. He, too, liked storms. When the thunder roared and the lightning flashed across the sky, Tom felt more alive than ever. It was as if all the earth was bellowing and bursting with life. And inside Tom was a kind of wild music keeping time with it all. But Tom never told his father about such feelings. Nor did he tell his mother. Father would have been alarmed, and Mother would have smiled and called it foolishness. Now Tom said, "I think the rain will at least help our crops. We haven't had a good rain in two weeks."

Becky continued looking out the window. "I am so pleased I can write," she remarked. "I think I will write a poem about the storm."

"Becky," Mr. Stockton reminded her, "you learned to read and write so you could read the Bible and write out your lessons."

"Oh, yes, Father, and I do," Becky said. "But I read the almanac too. In it are poems which I oft copy so that I might one day write poetry as well."

"Poetry is a frivolous undertaking," her father declared. "You must spend your time more wisely. When you become a wife and mother, the skills of cooking and sewing will serve you better than silly rhyming."

"Abel, leave the child alone," Mrs. Stockton finally said. "She is only 11 years old. Let her play at what she will. It can do no harm. I am sure God smiles on the fancies of children."

Tom was surprised to hear his mother speak so boldly. He knew that his father did not like anyone to disagree with him. Surely he would be annoyed that his wife had corrected him in front of the children.

Tom looked at his father and saw anger flare in his eyes. Then suddenly Mr. Stockton rose to his feet. "I'll be out checking on the fences and animal sheds," he said curtly.

"In the rain?" Mrs. Stockton asked in surprise.

But her husband turned and walked out of the room without answering. Tom could tell he was in a bad humor by the slam of the door.

Tom knew his father was worried about Becky's whimsical fancies. Aunt Odilia must have been like that when she was a child, Tom thought. Now, according to his father, Aunt Odilia had strange powers. Not that Tom believed it. It was all the power of suggestion. Tom had seen such things happen with his own eyes.

Once Schoolmaster Hopkins was teaching grammar to Tom's class. A troublesome boy named William was bored with the lesson. He began complaining that he was being sickened by a foul stench coming through the window.

Almost instantly other boys held their noses as well and cried, "The smell! We cannot stand it!" One very excitable boy actually swooned, hitting the floor with a great crash. Another vomited. And it was all because one boy had lied to relieve the boredom of grammar class.

More than likely, the same thing had occurred between Tom's father and Aunt Odilia. Odilia had probably told her brother that she could stick him with pins from afar, and he had believed her. That's all it was, Tom was sure—the power of suggestion.

While Mr. Stockton was still outside petulantly stomping about in the rain, Becky asked Tom, "Do you think it's possible to prophesy the weather, Tom?"

"Yes, I think so," Tom said. "By studying nature, Grandfather could tell when a storm was coming. He said a red sky in the morning means rain. And a red sky at night means the day will be clear."

"I'm keeping a record of my own weather lore," Becky explained, smiling proudly. "I'm looking very carefully at the fur on animals and at caterpillars. I'm excited to find out if I am any good at prophesying the weather."

"Aunt Odilia oft says that dew on a spider's web means a spell of good weather," Tom offered.

Becky's grin widened. "Oh, I must write that down. I've not heard that before. What else, Tom?"

"A red moon means wind," Tom recalled. "Uncle Nehemiah related a lot of weather lore to Aunt Odilia."

"A red moon!" Becky said. "Yes, I think

the moon had a reddish cast last night! What else?"

As Tom passed on his Aunt Odilia's wisdom to his sister, the rain turned heavier. It sounded as if someone were dumping a bucket of water on their small house.

A few minutes later, Mr. Stockton came in, shaking the water off his hat and coat. He glanced nervously at the ceiling as if he expected it to cave in at any moment.

"Come, let's eat," Mrs. Stockton announced. "I have made you some hot porridge, Abel. It will make you feel better."

The family sat quietly around the table, eating their meal. Suddenly they heard a knocking at the door above the noise of the storm. When Mr. Stockton went to answer it, he saw Edward Palmer, Agatha's father, standing before him.

"Come in at once, Edward," Mr. Stockton said. "What has happened? You look as if you've seen death!"

"Worse!" the man cried, entering the house. His clothing was soaked to the skin, and his dark hair lay in strands across his forehead. "It is Agatha, my daughter. She's been running around and hurling herself at furniture ever since she returned home this afternoon. She's screaming words with no meaning and swearing that a face at the window is bewitching her. We called Dr. Brewster at once."

Abel Stockton's eyes grew wide. "And what, pray tell, has the doctor to say of this?" he asked.

"That Agatha is afflicted by a malevolent spirit!" Mr. Palmer cried.

"No!" Mr. Stockton gasped. "Witchcraft?"

"Yes, and my poor wife is beside herself with grief," Mr. Palmer went on. "We have racked our minds to discover who would have a grievance against us to cause our child to be afflicted so."

Tom and the other children had been listening in silence, but now Becky said, "I remember sometimes when we studied our numbers at school, Agatha would be vexed sorely by a problem. She would have fearful tantrums. Once she even ripped her handkerchief with her teeth."

SPRING HIGH SCHOOL LIBRARY

Her father cast her a harsh look. "Silence, child! Your prattling has nothing to do with the matter at hand."

But despite her father's command, Becky continued. "And Miriam Dow was just as bad. The two of them would make such a fuss that Schoolmaster Hopkins would have to stop his lessons."

Mr. Stockton cast Becky another dark look, and she finally fell silent. He turned to Mr. Palmer then. "Does your daughter have a thought as to who the witch is?" he asked.

Mr. Palmer shook his head. "She will not say. When we ask her, she only clenches her teeth."

Mr. Stockton exchanged an anguished look with his wife. Tom knew what questions were going through his father's mind. Was Odilia Prescott responsible for Agatha's suffering? Had her strange and frightening ways finally led to this calamity?

Abel grasped Mr. Palmer's hand and said, "Have courage, Edward. At Meeting, we shall all pray for Agatha's deliverance from this curse."

But Mr. Palmer would not be soothed. "The witch must be found, Abel. At all cost! It is not only the fate of our child that hangs in the balance. All of Northboro could suffer grievous misfortune. Babes will be born dead. Animals will perish in the fields. Our crops will dry up and be blown away. We must find the witch, and she must be destroyed!"

"If there's a witch in Northboro, she will be found, Edward," Mr. Stockton assured him. "Of that you can be sure."

"Now I must go home to my wife and child," Mr. Palmer said. "I only thought it was important to tell you what has happened, you being our nearest neighbors. Good-bye."

"Good-bye, Edward," Mr. Stockton said. "Take heart. Surely Agatha will get better."

After Mr. Palmer had gone, Becky helped her mother clear the table. "I shouldn't be surprised if Aggie has made all this up," she said. "There was a peddler from the West Indies in town a fortnight ago. He told all kinds of wild stories of magic. I'm sure that's where Aggie got all her ideas."

"Becky, do not take such things so lightly lest you be afflicted yourself," her father warned.

Becky shrugged her shoulders and continued to help her mother.

"Sophie," Mr. Stockton said in a grave voice. "What do you make of this? Do you think there is a witch in Northboro? Or perhaps, might a witch have passed through and afflicted the girl?"

"Ah, Abel," his wife replied, "I put little stock in the prattling of Agatha Palmer. I have known her since she was born, and she has always been troublesome. There are no witches in Northboro. I have lived on this earth for 34 years and have yet to see one. And I never expect to."

Mr. Stockton grasped his head as if his anxiety caused him pain. "Sophie, you know the odd ways of my sister, Odilia. Do you think . . ."

"That Odilia's a witch? Never! She is a God-fearing woman," Mrs. Stockton said firmly.

"But I have told you how, when we were children, she could punish me with pinpricks from across the room. It happened many times," her husband insisted. "Sophie, I am sorely afraid that Odilia's strange ways are known to others in Northboro. And that could cause the villagers to suspect that she is the witch. If such a calamity should occur, it will cast a shadow over this entire family. I have heard of a wife who was accused of being a witch. And the husband and children were dragged into it as well. Our whole family would be imperiled." His breath was coming in rapid little gasps now.

"Abel, do not become so worked up," Mrs. Stockton gently scolded, handing her husband a cup of hot tea. "No one in Northboro shall ever accuse your sister of being a witch. It is a groundless fear."

But her husband was not convinced. He turned to Becky and said, "I forbid you to visit your Aunt Odilia again."

"But, Father, she has so many wonderful treasures in her house," Becky protested. "She has marvels from all over the world. I look on them and try to imagine life in those faraway places."

"You must not go there again," her

father cried. "If my sister is accused, you will be tarred with the same brush, child!"

Becky sighed. "Yes, Father," she said. Then she left the room and went outside. Tom followed her. The rain had stopped, and a great round disc of a moon cast its pale gold light on the yard.

"You know, Tom," Becky said, "that strange man from the West Indies said that witches have dolls that resemble people. So when a witch punishes a doll, the person it's made to resemble suffers too. What do you think of that?"

"How should I know?" Tom replied. "You know that Father forbids poppets or dolls of any kind in this house."

"Aunt Odilia has dolls," Becky said, lowering her voice.

A chill went through Tom's bones. He had often seen his aunt's collection of trinkets from around the world. But he had never seen any dolls among them. "Are you sure, Becky?" he asked.

Becky nodded. "Oh, yes, I have played with them," she said. "They're very pretty."

Tom grasped his sister's shoulders

firmly and held her fast. "Becky, listen to me. You must tell no one about Aunt Odilia's dolls, do you understand?" he said.

Becky looked surprised at Tom's earnestness. "I will say nothing, Tom. But I cannot see the harm in little dolls."

"Not a word of it, Becky," Tom warned, "or Aunt Odilia could suffer great harm!"

3 After chores the next morning, Tom climbed onto his horse and rode to Odilia Prescott's farm. He found her in the chicken yard scattering corn among the chickens.

Odilia was in her mid-forties, several years older than Tom's father. She was a plain-looking woman, almost homely. She wore her long, dark hair in a bun at the nape of her neck like most of the women of Northboro. But unlike them, she favored bright bonnets, especially green ones that complemented her eyes.

As Tom approached, she looked up with a big smile and hailed him. "Well, hasn't the rain put a bright face on the earth?" she called.

"It surely has," Tom said, dismounting. "And how are you, Aunt Odilia?"

"Fine, fine," the older woman replied as they walked together toward the house. "What brings you out here again today, Tom?"

Tom didn't quite know what to say. How could he bring up the subject of witchcraft? But he knew he had to. If hysteria was spreading, his aunt needed to be on the alert. She must be cautious about what she said or did.

"Aunt Odilia," Tom began as they reached the porch, "have you heard about what happened to Agatha Palmer?"

"No, and I don't need to," Aunt Odilia said decisively. "Those Palmers are dreadful. Never saw two more gloomy people in my life. And that daughter of theirs—"

"Aunt Odilia," Tom interrupted, "Agatha is why I came. She's been acting strangely—"

"Ha! I'm not surprised, what with those parents," Aunt Odilia snorted.

"Agatha has been throwing herself about and screeching meaningless words. And complaining that she is beset by a witch!" Tom blurted out. "Dr. Brewster says she is afflicted by an evil spirit."

"Indeed," Aunt Odilia snapped. "And pray tell me when did Dr. Brewster take leave of his senses? That girl needs more attention from her parents. And if that fails, a good sound whipping would cure her of such dangerous fancies."

"There's a lot of talk of witches here in

Northboro, Aunt Odilia," Tom continued. "It has happened like this in other villages with dire results. There have been trials and even hangings."

Aunt Odilia paused. She squinted her eyes and looked into her nephew's face. "Tom, what are you saying?" she demanded to know.

"Well . . ." Tom stammered, "it's just that . . . suspicion often settles on a woman who is alone and . . . plain-spoken. And Father worries that . . ."

Aunt Odilia began to laugh, and her green eyes shone. "That I'm a witch? Oh, your poor foolish father! He still clings to that childhood game we played, when I caused him to imagine he was pin-stuck!" She winked at Tom then and said, "Power of suggestion, my boy. Power of suggestion."

"That's not all, Aunt Odilia," Tom went on. "Becky said something else that has me worried. You well know that the laws of Northboro forbid us to have dolls in our houses. But Becky said you have some. It would be dangerous if anyone knew of this, because then surely they would have suspicions."

"Come inside, Tom. I'll show you my dolls," Aunt Odilia said. "You can see how harmless they are."

She led the way upstairs into the tiny bedroom where she kept her trinkets from around the world. All were brought home by Uncle Nehemiah. Aunt Odilia went to a small cupboard and withdrew a pair of bronze creatures that resembled elves. They were about two and a half inches tall with pointy hats and long beards.

"Nehemiah brought these from Wales," Aunt Odilia said. "He exchanged them for indigo and tobacco. He told me they were from Viking treasures."

Tom stared at the strange little pointy-hatted bronze figures. They surely did not look like Agatha Palmer!

"Well, those who fear witches think that a doll is made to resemble someone," he said. "And that a witch can torment the person by abusing the doll."

"Nonsense!" Aunt Odilia replied. "Don't trouble yourself over such things, Tom.

We weary our minds too much over nonsense. It takes energy from what should be our true purpose in life— becoming noble souls."

Tom smiled, encouraged. He thought Aunt Odilia was the wisest of all his relatives. He admired the way she supported herself, selling eggs and chickens. Sometimes a pig, or sometimes one of her marvelous multicolored quilts. When Uncle Nehemiah was lost at sea, she had made use of all her resources to survive.

"Well, Aunt Odilia, just take care not to unduly alarm anyone," Tom said as he mounted his horse to leave.

"Ha!" Aunt Odilia laughed, "I have been alarming folks all my life. I'm not about to stop now."

When Tom got home, three neighbor women were milling around his mother's kitchen. They had distressing news. Miriam Dow, one of the few friends Agatha Palmer had, was now also afflicted.

"My daughter cries out at night and speaks of seeing red and black cats clawing at her feet," Mrs. Dow cried.

"Oh, dear, Anne," Tom's mother said. "Perhaps the tales Aggie has been telling have caused your daughter to have bad dreams. I remember when I was a child and the boys would frighten me with stories of large snakes in the garden. I would oft awake crying in fear. But it was just a nightmare."

"I fear it is much more than that," Anne Dow lamented. "Miriam is afflicted while awake. And she believes she knows the source of her torment. A fortnight ago, she accidentally trod upon some flowers growing at Dorcas Manwell's door, and the old woman cursed my daughter."

Tom knew Dorcas Manwell. Everyone in the village knew her. She had many aches and pains which made her cranky and ill-tempered. She cherished few things as much as her pansies and peonies growing near her door. Gardening was one of the few pleasures left to her in life, she had once told Tom.

Tom had seen children deliberately stomp on her flowers just to bring the old woman outside. She'd brandish her broom and screech in her crackly voice, "Away with you, you little devils!"

If anyone in Northboro fit the description of a witch, Tom knew it was Dorcas Manwell. But he was sure that she was just a harmless old woman.

Now he said, "Surely Widow Manwell has not harmed a soul in her life by hand or by curse. She is faithful on Meeting Day, coming both to morning and afternoon services."

Immediately Mrs. Dow reprimanded him. "Tom Stockton, you are not sure of anything," she said. "You are a boy with a simple way of looking at things. You cannot fathom the evil intent of a dark spirit prowling among us. My daughter has said Dorcas Manwell cursed her, and I believe her. I would not be surprised should Dorcas Manwell prove to be the witch afflicting Agatha Palmer as well!"

"When have you ever seen Dorcas Manwell do harm to anyone?" Tom argued.

Tom's father laid a firm hand on his son's arm. "Do not defend her, Thomas," he said. "If she be a witch, no good person is to stand with her."

"But she's not a witch!" Tom snapped. "That's plain foolishness!"

Mrs. Dow paused and looked at Tom strangely. Then she said to her two friends, "Come along. We've much to attend to."

When they were gone, Mr. Stockton turned to Tom. "Take care you never speak on behalf of a witch in that way again. You are putting yourself and your family in grave danger. To speak in defense of witches makes you in sympathy with their evil works."

Tom looked at his mother. Now she, too, looked concerned. "Your father is right," she said. "Say no more to anyone concerning Dorcas Manwell."

Six-year-old Ann had been listening intently. In her cautious way she asked, "What does a witch look like?"

Becky was the first to speak up. She seemed fascinated rather than frightened when she answered. "Well, they are supposed to have special marks on their bodies called 'witch's marks.' They can be blue or red."

"Becky!" her father cried. "You speak of

witches as if you were familiar with them! Where do you get such knowledge?"

Becky shrugged her shoulders and said, "I told you, Father. The West Indian peddler told the children about such matters. And one of them told me."

"Well," Mr. Stockton said, shaking his finger in Becky's face, "You are never to speak of such things, do you hear?"

"Yes, Father," Becky said, lowering her eyes.

Mrs. Stockton had begun making bread for the next day. As she kneaded the dough, she shook her head and said, "I cannot believe that poor Dorcas Manwell is a witch. I pray she is innocent and that all this blows over before others are made to suffer."

"I am not so sure as you that she is innocent," her husband said darkly. "Evil is afoot in Northboro, and I have long wondered about Dorcas Manwell. How she lives alone in that ill-kept house, shrieking threats at children."

Tom was surprised at his father's words. He had never before heard him speak ill of Widow Manwell. Then Tom realized what was going on. His father was joining the others in pointing the finger of suspicion at Dorcas Manwell. As long as they suspected the widow, they wouldn't suspect his sister, Odilia Prescott. If Aunt Odilia was suspected, her guilt would reflect upon him and his family. Mr. Stockton was obviously anxious for Dorcas Manwell to be proven the witch.

* * *

The next day, Becky was in the barn milking the cow. Tom was forking hay into the loft above her. As Tom hoisted a forkful of hay, he glanced out the barn door. Agatha Palmer and Miriam Dow were coming down the road. They both appeared perfectly normal. Tom watched as they came up the path leading to the barn.

"Have you heard that the witch has been found, Becky?" Agatha asked, spotting the girl inside. "It was through our doing that the evil one has been uncovered."

Becky was just finishing her task. Before she spoke, she carefully lifted the pail brimming with the white liquid. Then she set the pail aside so that the cow would not overturn it with her leg. Finally she looked up and said flatly, "Say what you will, but I do not believe there is any witch in Northboro."

"Indeed there is," Agatha countered. "And it is Dorcas Manwell. We passed her house, and she came out and waved her arms in the air at us. Presently neither Miriam nor I could stop our arms from flailing about, causing our shoulders to ache mercilessly. Then the old woman stomped her foot and brought terrible pain to our feet."

"Why would Dorcas Manwell do such a thing to you?" Becky asked.

"Because we stepped on her flowers. We laughed, and she swore she would curse us. And now she afflicts us sorely," Agatha explained. Then she lowered her voice and added, "But she is perhaps not the only witch. There may be others. Minister Waller has called us to talk about the witches. We are very important because we are the ones who will save Northboro from evil."

"Yes, a heavy burden rests upon us," Miriam agreed solemnly.

"But you are only girls like me," Becky scoffed. "How can you know who is a witch?"

"Minister Waller will bring anyone accused of witchcraft before us. If we suffer afflictions, then that person will be tried as a witch," Agatha said simply.

"But how is anyone to know you are not just pretending to suffer these afflictions of yours?" Becky demanded.

"Becky Stockton," Agatha said sternly, "what evil has made you say such a thing? Do you wish for the witches to continue afflicting us? Do you not know that witches can make crops fail and babies die? How dare you doubt us! Or are you *yourself* under the power of witches?"

Tom looked at Becky. Her eyes were wide open, and her face was flushed. Tom recognized that look of indignation. He knew she was about to tell Agatha and Miriam exactly what she thought of them and their "witches." That will lead to trouble for sure, he thought.

Becky opened her mouth to speak but Tom cut her off, saying, "Becky, come. It's time to take the milk into the house. I'll help you."

"But—" Becky began.

"*Now*, Becky!" Tom said firmly.

Reluctantly Becky grasped one side of the bucket handle. Tom took the other. As they headed toward the house, Tom turned around and saw Agatha and Miriam leaving. They were marching confidently down the path, as if they were the most important children in all of Massachusetts.

4 Tom's parents invited Martha Burnside's family to supper the next evening. They wanted to welcome the new chandler and his wife.

Mr. Burnside was a stout man with a great red beard that made him look much older than his 45 years. Louise Burnside was a slender, comely woman who spoke softly.

"How goes your new business?" Mr. Stockton asked Martha's father during the meal.

"I already have more work than I can handle," Mr. Burnside replied. "I'll be hiring an apprentice soon."

"Excellent," Mr. Stockton remarked. "We have much need of a good chandler here."

"And how are your crops faring this year?" Martha's father asked.

The conversation about business and farming continued among the adults. Tom and Martha sat quietly, eating their meal of roasted chicken and potatoes. Occasionally their eyes met, causing both to blush.

After the meal, Tom asked if he might show Martha the farm.

"Certainly," Mr. Burnside replied. "Martha loves farm life, don't you, daughter?"

"Yes, Father, I do," Martha said, wrapping a shawl around her shoulders.

"Our farm is one of the largest in Northboro," Tom said as they left the house. "Do you see the land south beyond where the fence ends? There is a creek running through it."

"Oh, yes. How pretty it is!" Martha said.

"Father has offered me that parcel of land when I marry," Tom said.

"Then surely you will prosper with such a fine start," Martha said, smiling at Tom.

Tom smiled back. "Perhaps," he said. "Do you have older brothers and sisters, Martha?" he asked. He knew she was the only one living at home.

"Three sisters," Martha answered. "They married when they were 16—my age now." Her cheeks flushed with color.

Tom had mixed feelings as he looked at Martha and the land he might one day own. He liked Martha more each day. And his own father had married at 17, an age Tom would soon reach. But something deep inside him rebelled against the thought of settling down and making his life in Northboro. He longed for something more. He could not imagine himself 18 years from now like his own father. A stern man hacking a living from Massachusetts' rocky soil, trembling at the prospect of a bad crop.

"So you like farm life, Martha?" Tom asked, remembering what her father had said.

"Yes, I lived on a farm until I was 10, and then we moved to town," Martha answered. "I have very fond memories of those years."

"Do you think you will live in Massachusetts all your life?" Tom asked the girl. "I mean to say the land west of here is richer, I have heard. And there are not so many rocks to break a plow."

Sometimes Tom imagined traveling west and looking at some of the places he'd heard of. What were they like? he wondered.

Martha frowned and said, "But there are wild tribes there. I should be frightened to death to live in some lonely clearing where we might be attacked."

"We have always gotten on well with the Narragansetts," Tom said. "In 1633 when the smallpox epidemic hit, my mother's relatives took in some of the orphaned Narragansett children."

Martha looked unconvinced. A cool wind came up as the sun began to set, and Martha drew her shawl more tightly around her shoulders. "Tom, you have a little farm with a creek running through it right here. I should think that would be enough for anyone."

Tom said nothing. Maybe she's right, he thought. But I'm not ready to make that commitment yet. He decided that at another time he'd raise the subject again with Martha. Surely she could be convinced that there was a better, fuller world beyond Northboro.

They had reached the edge of the Stockton property, which was bordered by thick woods. Over the years, the Stocktons had worn a path through the woods for berry picking. The moon appeared now, casting long shadows across the path.

Tom was just about to remark how fair

the evening was when an animal appeared out of the woods. It stood on the path for an instant, watching them. Martha gasped. But as fast as it had appeared, the animal darted off into the brush. Tom had not had a chance to see what it was.

"Was that a feral cat?" Martha asked.

"I don't know," Tom admitted. "Probably—or a skunk."

"But it looked entirely black, Tom," Martha pointed out. "I saw no sign of white."

"There's no harm in a cat, no matter what color it is," Tom said. "They're good for controlling vermin."

"Tom!" Martha cried in a hushed voice. "Look!"

A dark figure wrapped in a black shawl emerged from the woods. Then it headed down the path, away from Tom and Martha.

"That's the old woman everyone is saying is a witch, isn't it?" Martha gasped.

"That's Dorcas Manwell, but she is no witch," Tom said.

"How are you so sure, Tom?" Martha said as the woman disappeared into the woods. "No sooner had the black cat entered the woods than the old woman emerged—as if she had transformed herself. It is said that witches traffic with spirits in the forests."

"I think that is a far-fetched idea, Martha," Tom said.

"But what if it be true? If she is indeed a witch, imagine what terrible things she could cause to happen in Northboro," Martha worried.

Tom smiled and turned to Martha. "Minister Waller will talk to the girls and get it all straightened out. He is a fine man, and he will discover the truth."

"But the minister is so very young," Martha said. "My father wonders at the wisdom of so young a man . . ."

"Minister Waller gives stirring sermons beseeching the people to amend their lives," Tom countered. "He encourages us to live by the Bible and avoid wickedness. The young minister is more apt to remind us of the darkness we make in our own lives than that caused by imaginary beings."

"Tom Stockton, you sound much like a

minister when you speak so," Martha said. "Perhaps that is your calling. And your words do settle my fears, I must say."

Tom smiled and walked the girl back to the house.

After the Burnsides went home, Tom's parents could not say enough in praise of Martha.

"Martha Burnside is truly a pearl of great value," Mr. Stockton said. "She reminds me of the good women spoken of in the Bible." He glanced at Tom then and added, "A young man would indeed be blessed to have her by his side through life."

"She is very pleasing in every way," Tom's mother agreed.

"Thomas, I couldn't help but notice that you spent much time with her," Mr. Stockton observed. "Does Martha Burnside please you as well?"

"Indeed, I have never met a girl who pleased me more," Tom said. He noticed that his remark made his parents smile.

The next day, Minister Waller asked some men of Northboro, including Tom and his father and Josiah Fezwelder, to join him at the meetinghouse for an inquiry. Also attending were the Dows and the Palmers.

Tom was nervous about the meeting. He had never had anything to do with legal proceedings in the town, nor had his father. But Mr. Fezwelder had once told Tom that he had been on a jury that had tried and convicted a witch in Andover. The old man seemed proud to have played a part in ridding Andover of such an evil. Tom hoped never to be asked to serve on such a jury.

As Tom and his father approached the meetinghouse, they saw Minister Waller coming down the lane. "You go on in, Father," Tom said. "I'm going to wait to say good morning to the minister."

Mr. Stockton nodded and went inside.

"Good morning, Minister," Tom said.

"Good morning, Tom," the minister answered.

Tom noticed that the young man looked worried.

"How is Dorcas Manwell?" Tom asked.

Mr. Waller lowered his voice. "She is here today," he said. "I have asked her to wait in a different room than the one we'll be meeting in. But it is my hope that we can settle this matter without a confrontation between her and the two— accusers."

"Will you allow the widow to speak to her own innocence?" Tom asked.

"I am hoping that it won't come to that," Waller answered. "I pray that the girls' antics will become apparent to all present. But if necessary, I will let the accused speak."

"I am relieved to hear that," Tom said, "for I believe this thing is the antics of the two girls."

Minister Waller clapped him on the shoulder. "Take heart, Tom. I'll try not to let this madness get out of hand."

Inside the meetinghouse, the parents of the afflicted girls hovered over them protectively. Miriam whimpered and clung to her mother. Agatha sat in a chair between Mr. and Mrs. Palmer. She had a pouty look on her face, as a child gets who has not had enough attention.

"Our task this morning is to decide if justices need be called to Northboro to hold a formal inquiry," Minister Waller said to the group. "This would be a serious move indeed. I am praying that we shall find another explanation for the girls' suffering and that we might resolve it. Now let us begin by—"

"Where is she?" Agatha suddenly cried out, cutting off the minister. "I know she is here! Where have you concealed the Widow Manwell?"

Agatha's father placed his arm around her shoulders to quiet her.

The minister looked surprised by Agatha's outburst. "My dear child—" he began in a soothing voice.

But Agatha clenched her teeth and struggled out from under her father's hold. "She is here, tormenting me!" she shrieked.

Now Minister Waller looked confused. Tom could see that he hadn't expected this. Tom felt sorry for the young minister. At Meeting, he spoke a stirring three-hour sermon urging people to live blameless lives. He cared for the sick until all hours of the night and comforted the troubled. But how could any of that have prepared him for this?

"Agatha," Minister Waller began again, "do you know how sinful it would be to accuse someone of witchcraft if that person was not guilty?"

Mr. Palmer lurched forward in his chair. "Minister! *My child* is the innocent one being tormented by a wicked spirit!" he cried.

Miriam Dow whimpered louder and cowered against her mother.

"Are *you*, Minister Waller, in league with the witch?" Mr. Palmer continued.

"Yes, tell us, Minister, are you a wolf in sheep's clothing trying to lead the people of Northboro astray?" Mr. Dow demanded.

At this remark, Minister Waller looked genuinely frightened. Tom could feel the tenseness in the room. It's all going wrong, he thought as he looked around. The people the minister had hoped to convince were now accusing *him* of witchcraft!

Tom saw Minister Waller glance at a closed door at the other end of the room. Tom knew that Dorcas Manwell was on the other side of that door. He wondered if the minister would still give her a chance to defend herself. But he could see that the rage in the eyes of the parents was discouraging the minister from summoning her.

But just then Dorcas Manwell came through the door unbidden and shouted, "You vile children are telling lies about me, are you not? You stomped upon my flowers and mocked me. And now you lie about me! Woe to you, you wicked little wenches!"

"Ayyyyeeeee," Agatha screeched, hurling herself to the floor and almost knocking Minister Waller over. "She's biting me! She's biting me!"

"You liar!" the widow thundered. "You are creating a performance to trap me!"

Tom couldn't stand it any longer. Something had to be done to expose Agatha Palmer's ridiculous act. He was just about to speak out when Miriam Dow dropped from her chair onto the floor.

Now both girls were tumbling about the room in high hysteria, clenching their teeth one moment and screaming the next. Agatha crashed into a chair and then howled, "Ohhh, she's burning me! Make her stop! Whenever she looks on me I'm in pain! Make her stop, make her stop!"

"Leave the room, Dorcas Manwell!" Minister Waller ordered. "Go at once!"

Dorcas Manwell sneered and stomped out of the room. The moment she was gone, the girls quieted down and rested quietly in their mothers' arms. Mr. Palmer was the first to speak. He pointed a bony finger at the minister. "Dorcas Manwell is a witch. No righteous man here would think otherwise. And you are not worthy to be our minister if you do not have her arrested and brought before a court of law!"

5 The townsmen and the others left, leaving only Tom, his father, and Mr. Fezwelder. Minister Waller sat in his chair, his face in his hands like a man stricken with a deathly illness. His flesh was pale, and he trembled.

Mr. Fezwelder said, "Minister, you must call for the justices. Dorcas Manwell must be prevented from causing further harm."

The young minister wrung his hands nervously. "I . . . I am as alarmed as you are, Josiah," he began, looking up at the older gentleman. He paused for a moment, then took a deep, shaky breath and continued. "But I am not convinced that those girls are sincere in their suffering. I detected in their eyes a glint of mischief just now."

"What are you saying, Minister?" Mr. Fezwelder demanded, glaring at the young man before him.

"It's just that I cannot . . . cannot but wonder if those girls created this entire thing as a diversion," Minister Waller replied. He looked hopefully around the room, as if searching for an ally.

Abel Stockton cleared his throat. For a

moment, Tom's heart lifted as he thought his father was about to speak in support of the minister. But then Mr. Stockton lowered his eyes and looked down at his hands. He continued to sit silently. Tom glanced at Mr. Fezwelder, who was still glaring at the minister.

The only ally the minister has is me, Tom thought. He decided to speak up, even though he knew his father would disapprove. "My sister, Becky, knows them well," he offered, "and she says the same thing."

Mr. Stockton looked up in shock at Tom's comment. He threw a warning glance at his son, but Tom continued.

"When their teacher asked them to study a subject they didn't like, they threw tantrums instead," Tom said. "One time Agatha ripped a handkerchief apart with her teeth, so great was her vexation at being made to recite her numbers."

"Nonsense!" Mr. Fezwelder interjected. "That behavior has nothing to do with what we saw here today." He turned to Minister Waller. "I fear we are going down the wrong road, Minister," he warned. "We are ignoring the presence of a witch in Northboro. And we shall ignore her to our sorrow. Shall we wait until our children are born dead and our cows no more give milk? Shall we wait until we are totally in the thrall of darkness and evil?"

Minister Waller shook his head and sighed. "I shall pray with all the fervor at my command to make the right decision," he promised. He stood up to indicate that the meeting was over. "Thank you for coming," he said.

Tom and his father bade the minister and Mr. Fezwelder good-bye and headed home.

"Thomas," Mr. Stockton said when they were out of earshot. "Whatever made you speak so? Your words may well have put us all in danger."

"I am convinced that hysteria is starting to grip this village, Father," Tom said. "And I cannot go along with it. The fear of witches will cause people to suspect their friends, their neighbors—even their relatives of witchcraft."

Tom saw his father flinch and knew the older man was thinking of Aunt Odilia.

"If this is allowed to continue," Tom

went on, "innocent people will be condemned. Their families will be left destitute. I cannot in good conscience allow that to happen."

"But you will incriminate us, Tom," Mr. Stockton said.

"I will indeed try my best not to, Father," Tom said. "It is my hope that this madness can be stopped before it comes to that."

Mr. Stockton said nothing but sat in silence for the rest of the ride home.

A few days later, Tom was invited to the Burnsides' home. When he arrived, Martha took him into the parlor, where her parents were waiting. Mrs. Burnside served everyone a cup of hot tea.

"What are your skills, Thomas?" Mr. Burnside asked almost immediately, as if he were sizing Tom up as a husband for his daughter.

"I am a farmer and a fair carpenter," Tom said.

"Honorable work," Mr. Burnside remarked. "Are you satisfied with it?"

"Sometimes I am," Tom said.

"Perhaps you would like to learn the art

of candle making," Mr. Burnside offered. "I am soon in need of a bright young apprentice, you know."

"I am not sure what work I will pursue," Tom said. "I had an uncle who was a seafaring man. Sometimes I feel the lure of faraway places."

Mr. Burnside frowned. "That is not work for a married man," he said.

Tom glanced at Martha. She looked disappointed by his remark and stared forlornly into her teacup. Tom hastily added, "But I may not go to sea. To a young boy, it seems an inviting thing. But a man must take life more seriously."

"Indeed so," Mr. Burnside said. Martha brightened noticeably. "Consider becoming a chandler, Thomas. It is far less dangerous than the sea and more dependable than farming. It does not rely on the weather to turn a profit. A worthy trade, don't you agree?"

Tom nodded and smiled outwardly, but inside he felt turmoil. The idea of spending his life forming hot wax into candles held less appeal for him than farming.

Later Tom and Martha took a walk

through the village. Tom noticed that it took but a few minutes to pass from one end of the main street to the other. He found himself wondering what a large city like Boston would be like. Aunt Odilia had said that the streets of Boston were teeming with people. And one could buy many things that people in Northboro never even dreamed of.

"Martha, have you ever been to Boston?" he asked.

"No. I've not been more than 20 miles from Northboro. The last village we lived in is only about 15 miles from here," Martha said.

"I have not seen Boston either," Tom said, "but I should like to. It has docks and wharves and foreign ships. I have heard there are as many as 6,000 people in Boston."

"Six thousand!" Martha said. "That is an astonishing number. I would be frightened by so many people."

"Martha, are you never curious about other places?" Tom asked.

"Curious? No," Martha replied. "I am content to be surrounded by people who know me and think as I do. It is as if we all belong to a huge family."

Faint annoyance crept into Tom's voice. "Martha, Dorcas Manwell has lived here all her life, and she has never harmed a soul. Yet some of her neighbors now attempt to have her charged with witchcraft. I think it would be more comforting to live among strangers if my neighbors were such!"

"Tom, have you ever wondered if maybe she *is* a witch? If that be so, then her neighbors have no choice but to put an end to her," Martha said.

"She's not!" Tom snapped. "Those silly girls have told lies. It is a cruel and vicious thing to arrest an old woman over such nonsense. Dorcas Manwell might not be the most pleasant person in Northboro. But she's certainly not a witch!"

Martha's eyes welled with tears. "Oh, Tom, I have upset you, and I am sorry. Are you angry at me?"

Tom looked at the sad, lovely face and regretted his harsh words. He smiled and replied, "No, I am not angry at all."

Tom walked Martha home then. Before she went inside, Martha turned and smiled at Tom. "Good-bye, Tom," she said in a voice filled with affection.

"Good-bye, Martha," Tom replied.

As he headed home, he thought about the idea of marrying Martha. She is kind and beautiful and eager to do the right thing, he told himself. And she loves me, of that I am sure. There could be no more suitable wife for me.

And yet Martha was like a lovely flowering bush growing firmly rooted in Massachusetts' soil. And Tom was like a seabird with salt air in its lungs. He didn't know if such a marriage would ever take place.

When Tom got home, he found his mother had taken Becky, Ann, and Samuel with her to visit a neighbor. His father was working on the north end of their land, too far from the house to be seen.

Eight-year-old Elizabeth sat on the front steps of the house, a coal black cat on her lap. Tom was startled to see the strange cat curled up on his sister's lap, purring contentedly.

"Elizabeth, why didn't you go with Mother and the others?" Tom asked.

"I wanted to stay here with Miss Molly," Elizabeth answered, nodding at the cat on her lap. "That's what I named her. Isn't she a pretty cat, Tom?"

"Yes. Where did she come from?" Tom asked. Most the farm cats in the area were gray or yellow tabbies. Tom had never seen a black cat around. Unless it was the one that darted across the path the other night when he was with Martha.

"I don't know. I saw her at the edge of the woods," Elizabeth replied. "She followed me home, and I gave her some milk. I talk to her, and I think she understands me a little. I understand her too."

"Is that so?" Tom asked, amused. "And what does Miss Molly say?"

"That she has had a hard life," Elizabeth replied. "She was born in the woods, and once she had three brothers and sisters and a mother. But they all went away, and she's been very lonely ever since."

Tom sat down beside his sister. "And she told you all this?" he asked.

"Yes," Elizabeth said.

"Elizabeth, you must not tell stories," Tom said. "The cat cannot talk, so she did not tell you anything. You made all this up, didn't you?"

Elizabeth giggled. "Yes," she admitted. "I'm sorry, Tom." She stroked the cat some more and added, "Miriam Dow came by a little while ago. She looked at my cat and said it was a witch's cat."

"Elizabeth, you must not talk to Miriam Dow or Aggie Palmer anymore. They are wayward girls," Tom said.

"I don't like them either," Elizabeth said. "Miriam said she hopes my cat dies. And I told Miriam I would get even with her for saying such a cruel thing."

Tom was surprised by his shy sister's threat. "Elizabeth, how would you get even with Miriam?" he asked.

Elizabeth reached into her sewing basket and removed a tiny corn husk doll. "The West Indian peddler told my friends that if you make a doll to look like a person who vexes you, you can stick a pin into the doll and—"

"Elizabeth!" Tom cried, snatching the doll from Elizabeth. "You must never do such a thing again. It's wicked! If Father saw what you did, he would whip you sore. What has gotten into you?"

Elizabeth bit her lip to keep back the tears. Clutching the cat, she ran behind the house to escape her brother's frightening anger.

Tom stared down at the doll in his hand. He wanted to burn it quickly, but there was no fire in the hearth. As he was debating what to do, he heard someone close by.

"Thomas Stockton!" a girlish voice called.

Tom turned to see Miriam Dow standing at the gate. Obviously she had not gone home after talking to Elizabeth. She had probably hidden in the trees. "Thomas Stockton," she said, "what is that you have in your hands?"

"Go home, Miriam," Tom snapped. "Your parents will be worrying about you."

"You have a doll, don't you?" Miriam accused. "I saw it. You took it from Elizabeth, didn't you? Your sister is a witch, isn't she? *Isn't she?*"

6 Tom's mind raced. How could he get rid of the doll? He quickly squashed it in the palm of his hand until it looked like no more than the ruins of a corn husk. Then he scattered the shreds into the air and said, "I was eating a cob of corn, and this is what I peeled off. Would you have me eat the husks, Miriam? You shall be the laughingstock of Northboro if you cannot tell a husk of corn from a doll!"

Miriam fell silent, her lower lip thrust forward in disappointment. Tom had convinced her that she had been mistaken. But she said in a sullen voice, "I *did* see the black cat, and I *do* believe it's a witch."

"It is a cat, a simple cat," Tom said. "It drinks milk and mews. You are a very foolish girl. Now go home, Miriam, and stop troubling us."

Miriam turned slowly and started on the road toward home. She was clearly unhappy that she had not discovered a magic doll and a cat who was really a witch.

But Tom found himself shaken from the

experience. How easy it was to pass from innocent villager to accused witch! Even a child like Elizabeth wasn't safe. Tom had heard of a five-year-old in a nearby village who had been charged with witchcraft.

He went to search for Elizabeth. He found her sitting crouched against the chicken coop, crying softly. When she saw him approach, she hastily wiped her tears with the back of her hand. Then she deliberately looked in the opposite direction.

Tom knelt beside her. "Elizabeth, I'm sorry I was so harsh with you. Will you forgive me?"

Elizabeth sniffed a few times and wiped away a few more tears. Then she said, "I forgive you, Tom."

"Good. Thank you, Elizabeth," Tom replied. "But you must never, *ever* speak to Miriam or Agatha again, do you understand? And you must never make dolls from corn husks—or from anything else."

Elizabeth nodded obediently and said, "I'm sorry. I won't do it anymore."

Tom smiled at the little girl and hoisted

her upon his broad shoulders. He gave her a piggyback ride around the farm as he did his chores. Soon Elizabeth was laughing merrily from her perch on her older brother's shoulders.

* * *

In the morning the Stocktons received word that Minister Waller had left Northboro to accept a post in Pembroke Village. Evidently he had been "convinced" to leave by some very influential townspeople. The young minister, his wife, and their two young children left by night in a great hurry without bidding farewell to anyone.

The following Meeting Day, a new face appeared to deliver the sermon. Edward Carruthers, a fiery minister from a nearby village, had a gray, angular face and burning eyes that peered down a great hawk nose. The influential townspeople evidently deemed Carruthers to be better suited than Minister Waller to root out the witches in Northboro.

"You, the people of Northboro, have

brought upon yourselves a terrible judgment," Minister Carruthers thundered from the great pulpit at the front of the room. "I have been here only three days, and already I have seen much evidence of wickedness."

The parishioners responded to the new minister with frightened silence. Some of them shifted in uneasy guilt. They wondered if their misdeeds were the ones that had brought the witches.

"I have seen people sitting idly while homes and farms go untended," Minister Carruthers shouted. "I have witnessed men imbibing shamefully in liquors. I have seen women gossiping instead of going modestly about their duties. I have observed young people in wild and unseemly pleasures. It is no wonder that there is a plague of witches upon your village!"

The sounds of nervous coughing and throats clearing filled the room.

"Yes," the new minister cried, "there are witches in Northboro. More than one, it is certain. They now torment innocent children because of what evil adults have done. We must ferret out the witches and make an end to them at the gallows. And you must amend your lives so that witchcraft never again finds fertile soil in your village!"

The constable of Northboro arrived at Dorcas Manwell's house in the late afternoon. Tom did not see what happened, but his friend Peter did. He related the incident to Tom.

"It was terrible, Tom," Peter said. "At first the widow did not understand what was happening. She laughed and said it was all a mistake. But then they dragged her off in chains."

"What a wicked and unjust deed!" Tom said angrily.

"I could not believe they would treat a woman of that age so cruelly," Peter said. "And have you heard the latest rumors concerning the widow?"

"No," Tom said.

"You know that Dorcas Manwell was widowed and left childless by the smallpox epidemic," Peter said.

"Yes," replied Tom.

"Now it's being rumored that her family

didn't die of smallpox at all," Peter continued. "That she somehow did away with them. They're saying that she made a potion and poisoned them all."

Tom shook his head and sighed. "It is a pity she has no family to stand with her," he said.

"If she had a family and they defended her, they would only end up accused too," Peter pointed out. "It seems the only safe thing to do when family members are accused is to denounce them."

"But what person could do such a thing?" Tom cried.

Peter shrugged. "Who knows what one will do when the gallows casts its shadow?" he said. "I am only glad that none in my family is apt to fall under suspicion."

"Did they take the widow to the jail?" Tom asked.

"Yes. And she's to remain there while the justices make their way to Northboro," Peter replied.

"Who are the justices?" Tom wanted to know.

"Various men of reputation who have

presided at witch trials before," Peter answered. "They will study the evidence and then pass judgment."

"Heaven help poor Dorcas Manwell if the justices rely upon those two girls' testimony," Tom said.

"I have heard that the only way for a convicted witch to avoid the gallows is to accuse another," Peter commented. "It would not surprise me if Dorcas Manwell points to another poor soul to save her own neck."

Tom hadn't thought of that. Years ago the Widow Manwell and Aunt Odilia had a disagreement over some property they had both laid claim to. Aunt Odilia had won the case, and Dorcas Manwell bore her a terrible grudge. She had not spoken to Odilia Prescott since. How tempting it would be to save herself by calling her old adversary a witch! Tom thought.

Before the end of the week, a third child was showing signs of being bewitched. She was a tall, scrawny girl named Belinda, whose family was good friends with the Palmers. At first Belinda's performances were not as dramatic as those of the other two girls. But within a few days, her antics rapidly mimicked Agatha and Miriam's wildest convulsions.

Tom decided it was time to visit Aunt Odilia again. He wanted to warn her of what Dorcas Manwell might do at the trial.

Odilia was sitting on her doorstep staring up at the sky when he arrived. "Good evening to you, Tom," she called. "Did you know this is the best time to see the stars?"

"Yes," Tom replied as he approached the older woman. "You told me a long time ago that the best times are 30 minutes after sunset and 30 minutes before sunrise."

"You never forget, do you, Tom?" Aunt Odilia said, obviously pleased.

Tom joined his aunt on the step. "Aunt Odilia, did you know that they have taken Dorcas Manwell to prison and will bring her to trial for being a witch?"

"I have heard," Odilia replied dryly. "And it's madness—plain madness, I say. Dorcas is a cross old thing, but who wouldn't be with the aches and pains she suffers? The good God forgives her grumblings. Why can't these foolish people see her for what she is—a harmless old soul?"

"I pray she will be found innocent, but I have grave doubts," Tom said. "When those girls put on their show, they may well convince the justices."

"Those girls should be spanked soundly and fed only bread and water until they repent for their lies," Aunt Odilia said.

"Aunt, I've heard that it oft happens that when people are convicted of witchcraft, they seek to save themselves by naming others. In that way, they may be pardoned," Tom said. "I fear that Dorcas Manwell will seek to lay the blame on someone else if she is found guilty."

Aunt Odilia smiled wryly. "And who better to point the finger at than me?" she said. "The one who laid claim to that fat piece of land she wanted years ago."

"That has crossed my mind," Tom admitted.

"Well, they shall not charge me with witchcraft," Aunt Odilia said decisively. "I am a praying woman. I shall stand before my Creator one day with a clear conscience."

"I fear that doesn't matter," Tom said. "All that matters is that a person is accused. And then those girls may decide to carry on with a frenzy, and that is enough to send that person to the gallows. It is all in the hands of those wicked children to condemn whomsoever they choose."

"But what would you have me do, Tom?" Aunt Odilia asked.

"This," Tom said. "Have a bag packed with those things necessary to you, and keep a horse at the ready. I shall attend the hearings, and if things go badly and Dorcas Manwell accuses you, then I will come warn you. Then you must flee to Rhode Island."

"You want me to flee the house where I have lived for more than 25 years?" Aunt Odilia asked, her green eyes flashing in disbelief. "The house Nehemiah built with his own two hands? Tom, my hope is to leave this property to you one day. To use for whatever purpose you wish. Perhaps if you don't want to farm, you will sell it and buy a sailing ship. If I am condemned as a witch and I do not defend myself, my goods and property will be confiscated by the state. You know the law."

"Better to lose your property than your life," Tom remarked. "Better to lose it all. I cannot bear the thought of someone so dear to me being sent before an unjust court!"

"They will not dare accuse me," Aunt Odilia said as Tom mounted his horse again. "And if they do, I shall battle them mightily. And I shall triumph!"

Tom wheeled on his horse and looked back. "I beg you, Aunt. Pack what you need and be ready to ride. I swear to you I will bring a warning before it grows too late!"

7 On Monday, Schoolmaster Hopkins took all the children of Northboro on a scientific walk. He asked Tom and Peter to come along to help keep order. The teacher told the children that the purpose of the outing was to identify some of the plants and wildlife of the region. But Tom suspected it was to get the children's minds off the subject of witches. The hearings were to be held the next day, and the entire town was talking about them.

To Tom's surprise, all three girls who claimed to be afflicted came along.

"The evil witch who has been tormenting us is locked away," Agatha explained when someone asked them why they were there. "So she cannot cast her evil eye upon us."

"So there is just one witch?" Becky asked.

"We do not know," Miriam said. "Perhaps there are more. I just pray we find none today."

Schoolmaster Hopkins frowned at the conversation and said, "There shall be no talk of witches on this outing. Today we are to learn from nature."

The children gathered around a struggling white pine while Schoolmaster Hopkins explained why the soils of Massachusetts were generally poor. Then the group moved on, eventually passing Dorcas Manwell's house. Her chickens wandered about the yard in disorder. Dorcas Manwell had been taken away in such haste that she was not able to make any provisions for her animals.

"Look," Becky said, "there is Dorcas Manwell's little farm. How sad it looks."

"Do not have sympathy for a witch, Becky!" Agatha warned. "Or you, too, may be believed to be in league with the devil."

Once again Schoolmaster Hopkins scolded the girls. "Let us concentrate on scientific matters," he said. "Come along."

The group continued on its way past the widow's farm.

Suddenly a look of fear passed over Agatha's face.

"What is it, Aggie?" Miriam said.

"Look! In the upstairs window!" Agatha cried. "The witch stands there!"

Everyone looked at the window of

Dorcas Manwell's house. A woman's figure stood stiffly facing out.

"It's true!" Miriam shouted. "Dorcas Manwell is out of jail!"

"Ohhhh," Agatha screeched. She immediately fell to the ground and began clawing the earth like a wild animal. Miriam tumbled into the brush and ground her teeth. Belinda took some time longer to join in the uproar, being caught off guard. But soon she, too, was rolling about in the dust.

"This is madness!" Schoolmaster Hopkins shouted. "Stop it at once! I order you to compose yourselves!"

"Make her stop looking at me," Agatha screamed.

"She's biting me! She's biting me!" Miriam wailed.

"Stop this! Stop this shameful behavior at once!" the teacher demanded.

"They can't help it, sir," another girl said solemnly. "They are afflicted. The witch has put the evil eye on them."

As the group watched in horror, the girls continued to writhe and moan on the ground.

Suddenly Becky laughed out loud. "Look! That is not Dorcas Manwell in the window!" she said. "It's a dress form. The widow sews for some of the ladies in town."

Tom peered at the figure in the window. His sister was right. At first glance it looked like a woman. But upon closer inspection, one could tell that it was simply the form of a woman, used for fitting dresses.

The girls' antics stopped at once. Agatha got slowly to her feet, smoothing her tangled hair. Her dress had been torn by her thrashing about in the dirt. Miriam looked almost as bad. Belinda began looking for her bonnet that she had ripped off and hurled into the brush.

"You see?" Becky said for all to hear. "It is all trickery. There was no witch with an evil eye. The girls pretended to be afflicted. It is all a lie."

"A witch was afflicting us from somewhere," Agatha cried, looking up at the branches of the surrounding trees. "It must have been another witch!" She glared with hatred toward Becky.

"Stop this at once!" Schoolmaster Hopkins thundered. "I will not tolerate such behavior on my scientific walk. I have a willow whip here. And I will thrash the next child who speaks of witches!"

The children and teacher continued on their way. The three girls remained calm for the remainder of the morning. At noon, the group stopped in a shady grove for a picnic lunch. Afterward they were dismissed.

As Tom and Becky headed toward home, Agatha approached with the other two girls. "You deliberately tried to make fools of us in front of the group, did you not, Becky Stockton?"

"You proved yourself to be a fraud, Aggie. And you know it," Becky replied. "You are all fine liars. You'd better go to Mr. Carruthers before tomorrow and confess what you have done so that innocent people might not suffer on your account."

Indignation flared in Agatha's eyes. "That is not so! We *are* afflicted by witches. We are innocent children. Everyone in Northboro pities us. The witches must be caught and punished.

Beware, Becky Stockton, lest someone in *your* family be revealed as a witch!"

A chill went up Tom's spine.

"Your Aunt Odilia is a strange one," Agatha remarked. "It is not normal for a woman to live alone, so far removed from society."

"Odilia Prescott is a fine person," Tom cut in. "She is a praying woman who offers alms to the poor from the little she has."

"But she *is* strange," Agatha insisted. "And sometimes she roams about at night looking at the heavens. As if she is waiting for a stick to climb upon so she might ride across the face of the moon."

"It is so," Miriam added dutifully. "Odilia Prescott sometimes laughs to herself in unseemly ways. Witches do oft have laughing spells."

"And I heard she has little dolls," Belinda added.

"You would be wise to guard your wicked tongues," Becky warned, "before heaven punishes you!"

When the three girls left, Tom and Becky headed for home in another direction.

"I am much in fear of the lies of those

girls," Tom said. "They could easily throw suspicion on Aunt Odilia."

"But everyone saw them proved liars this morning," Becky said. "They cannot go on being believed forever. Surely someone will prove them false."

"One would hope so," Tom agreed. "But to accuse them of being false is to accuse oneself of being a witch. It is a dangerous business. And when danger arises, courage fails even the best of people."

* * *

The public hearing on Tuesday brought out a great crowd. Some came out of fear, anxious to see witchcraft stamped out. Others came out of curiosity. Still others did not want to miss the excitement. Nothing like this had ever happened in the sleepy little village of Northboro before— and might never happen again. They certainly did not want to miss it.

One by one, the justices arrived and seated themselves at their tables. They were dressed in flowing black cloaks and had a look of frightening seriousness about them. None cracked a smile, and all stared ominously at the crowd as if it were indeed full of witches.

A stout, dark-haired man with an unkind face walked in next.

"Who is that?" Tom asked his father.

"Mr. Landis," Mr. Stockton answered. "He's the lawyer from Boston hired to conduct the questioning."

Tom felt a tapping on his shoulder and turned around. It was Martha Burnside. She sat between her parents, who smiled at Tom.

"Hello, Martha," he said. Then he nodded at her parents and added, "Mr. and Mrs. Burnside."

As Tom turned back around, he noticed everyone staring toward the other end of the room. Dorcas Manwell was being brought in, her hands and feet in chains. The sight sickened Tom, and his heart went out to her. The old woman's head hung low, and she looked haggard. The days in prison had already taken a toll on her body and spirit.

"May the good Lord have mercy on the

souls of those wicked girls," Tom whispered to his father beside him.

"Watch your tongue, Thomas," Mr. Stockton cautioned. "Even a whisper can condemn you."

Mr. Landis approached Dorcas Manwell and said in a sharp, accusing voice, "Dorcas Manwell, do you understand the charge against you?"

Timidly the widow nodded.

"What say you to the charges?" Mr. Landis asked.

"I am innocent. I have done nothing wrong. If you think me a witch, you are sadly mistaken," Dorcas Manwell said.

"Is it true, Dorcas Manwell, that you live alone in your house with neither husband nor kin?" Mr. Landis asked.

"It is so. I am a widow. My husband and children perished in the smallpox outbreak more than 20 years ago," the woman answered.

"Is it true that you bear upon your body spots of sunken flesh from contact with an evil spirit?" the lawyer demanded.

"No, sir. I have no such wounds. All my infirmities are the result of old age," the woman said in a trembling voice. She was a far cry from the spirited, defiant woman she had been only days ago.

Tom clenched his hands in rage. Such a thing should not be happening in Northboro or anywhere else, he thought. Northboro had been settled by people who had fled England to escape just such injustice. And now the same thing was happening here.

"Dorcas Manwell, have you signed the book of the devil?" the lawyer demanded.

"No, sir," she said.

"Have you ever touched the book of the devil?" he asked.

"No, sir," the old woman said, shaking her head sadly.

"So you deny being in league with the devil?" Mr. Landis asked in an accusing voice.

"Yes, oh yes, I wholeheartedly deny it," Dorcas Manwell answered.

"Very well. Bring in the three afflicted children!" Mr. Landis ordered.

The three girls were brought in then. When she saw them, Dorcas Manwell dropped her head to her chest. She seemed too hurt by their accusations to look them in the eye.

Immediately Agatha clutched the back of her neck. "She is trying to break our necks!" she cried. Her companions did the same, coughing and gasping as they took hold of their own necks.

"Ohhhh," Miriam wailed, "I cannot breathe! I cannot breathe!"

Tom heard many people around him gasp. The children were obviously in terrible distress. In an instant they dropped to the floor, wailing pitifully and crying out, "Make her stop hurting us!"

Mr. Landis turned to the old woman and said, "Dorcas Manwell, I order you to raise your head."

Dorcas Manwell did as she was told. The moment she raised her head, the girls' torments ceased. They climbed back into their seats and cowered against their parents.

Mr. Landis stared at the widow and said, "Dorcas Manwell, I command you to tell me the truth. Have you ever signed the book of the devil?"

"No, never! Never!" Dorcas Manwell cried.

"But you *touched it!*" Mr. Landis shouted. "Tell the truth! For your lies will send you to the gallows. Only the truth and your repentance can save you now. Dorcas Manwell, *did you not touch the book of the devil?*"

8 Dorcas Manwell collapsed in her chair, too distraught to answer. "This is an outrage!" Tom whispered to his father.

Edward Carruthers, who was seated near the Stocktons, overheard Tom. He turned to Tom's father and said, "What say you to all this? What does your son mean by his outrage?"

"My son regrets that such trials need be in Northboro," Mr. Stockton hastily explained. "But my family and I condemn witchcraft in all its forms."

Minister Carruthers leaned around Mr. Stockton and stared icily at Tom for a long moment. Then he returned his attention to the trial.

"Remove the accused!" one of the justices ordered. The widow, head bent and sobbing, was taken to a nearby chair.

The questioning continued as Agatha Palmer was brought to the stand to give testimony. The tall, slim, dark-haired girl was the picture of a demure and righteous child. She presented a pitiable sight indeed to the sympathetic spectators .

"Agatha, have you ever been harmed by

Dorcas Manwell?" Mr. Landis asked in a kindly voice.

"Yes," Agatha replied, dabbing her eyes with a handkerchief.

"How many times has she harmed you?" the man asked.

Agatha's voice broke dramatically as she replied, "Many times."

"What did she do to you, Agatha?" Mr. Landis asked.

"She choked me and pinched me and bit me, sir," Agatha said, looking to her parents for support. Tom glanced at the Palmers. They were staring at Dorcas Manwell, their hard faces filled with hatred.

"Did this happen during the day or at night?" the lawyer questioned.

"It was most times during daylight, sir," Agatha said. "But sometimes she would peer into my window from the darkness outside and bewitch me."

A murmur of disapproval arose from the audience.

"Thank you, Agatha," Mr. Landis said. "You may sit down now."

Miriam and Belinda gave similar

testimonies. All the girls watched Dorcas Manwell closely from their places. She had but to move her foot, and they began to moan that their feet hurt. If she blinked, the girls wailed in unison that their eyes burned in their heads.

Tom pitied the old woman as she stared around the room at her neighbors and friends. The faces were closed and hostile toward her. She must feel as if she has not a friend in Northboro, he thought.

Mr. Landis had the widow brought to the stand again.

"Dorcas Manwell," he began, "confess your evil deeds now! Tell us all you know. If you were driven to these deeds by witches more powerful than yourself, speak their names now. And beg the mercy of this gathering that you might not die."

Tom stiffened. Now was the dangerous moment. Possibly Dorcas Manwell thought her only chance to save herself lay in accusing someone else. This would be the moment she would do so.

In a faltering voice, Dorcas Manwell admitted, "I confess that I touched the book of the devil. And I confess that I harmed the three girls."

Immediately the audience was on its feet.

"Hang her!" someone shouted.

"Send her back to the devil where she belongs!" another demanded.

The widow looked around in a panic. "Wait! Wait I tell you!" she cried. "Another forced me to do it! I swear!"

A collective gasp arose from the crowd, followed by a babble that the justices silenced. Everyone turned to look at the person on either side. Their eyes all asked the dreaded question, *If there be another witch in Northboro, who is it?*

"Speak, Dorcas Manwell," Mr. Landis commanded, his own eyes afire with excitement.

"Another brought me the devil's book and made me sign it," the old woman said. Her voice was the frightened, uncertain voice of a naughty child begging for forgiveness. "She signed it first, and I was bidden to do the same. But I would not until she afflicted me sorely. And then I was bidden to do dark deeds of magic. I did it from fear, I swear. I bore the girls no ill will, but I was bidden to afflict them and so I did."

More gasps followed. Excitement surged in the room like bolts of lightning from an electrical storm.

"Name the witch who bade you to afflict these children!" Mr. Landis thundered.

Dorcas Manwell struggled to her feet, her chains clanking, "It was Odilia Prescott," she cried. Then she fell back into her chair as if the enormity of her slander struck her like a blow.

Tom heard Martha gasp from behind him. For an instant, the room seemed to darken before his eyes. He'd never been so frightened. All his dread had come to pass. Forgetting the danger he was placing himself in, he cried out, "She lies! The widow lies!"

Tom's parents pulled him back down. Mr. Stockton stammered, "My son is overcome with grief! Forgive him for this outburst, for it comes from a broken heart. Events have unsettled him!"

Tom could feel all eyes in the room

upon him. Minister Carruthers leaned forward again, a look of shocked horror on his face. Mr. Landis glared at Tom but let the comment pass. "Remove the woman from the room," he said.

Dorcas Manwell rose from her seat and was led toward the door. As she left the room, her gaze met Tom's. She looked away quickly, her red-rimmed eyes narrow with shame.

But Tom did not hate her for what she had done. He knew that it was fear, not ill will, that had moved her. How many others would do the same? he wondered as he gazed around him.

Now the three girls were in a highly agitated state, recounting deeds of witchcraft related to Odilia Prescott.

"Odilia Prescott once crossed a muddy road without getting the hem of her dress soiled," Agatha cried. "I witnessed it myself."

Belinda nodded. "Now that I think of it, I saw her flying high above her barn one day!"

"Yes," Miriam agreed. "And I once saw a red garment hanging on her clothesline.

Red! Can you imagine? Everyone knows that red is the color of the devil."

Tom rushed from the meetinghouse with his parents close behind. "I must warn Aunt Odilia to flee!" he said.

"You must not go there!" Mr. Stockton cried. "They might find you when they go to fetch her. Then you, too, will be arrested!"

"Your father is right," Tom's mother pleaded. "Stay with us!"

But Tom broke free of his parents. "I'll be back to get you within the hour!" Tom called as he boarded the Stocktons' wagon and took hold of the reins. As he headed out of town, he glanced behind him. His parents' faces were filled with terror as if they might never see him again.

A quarter of an hour later, he reached the Prescott place. Tom leaped off his horse and pounded on the door with both hands. Aunt Odilia opened the door and looked at Tom.

"So the worst has come to pass?" she asked calmly.

"Yes, Dorcas Manwell has accused you,"

Tom said between gasps of breath. "She did it to save herself. The constable will be here any moment to take you. You must go at once. I will help you get your things in your wagon. Then you must be off to Rhode Island—at breakneck speed!"

Aunt Odilia planted her hands firmly on her hips and said, "I will not run from my house like a thief in the night!"

"You don't understand," Tom pleaded. "Those girls will condemn you. You will not be given a chance to prove your innocence. Aunt Odilia, I beg you to go!"

Odilia laid her hand on the boy's arm. "I am touched by your concern, Tom. But if I don't stay and defend my innocence, I convict myself of witchcraft. The greedy officials will steal this land. I refuse to give them the house that Nehemiah raised with loving hands and the land we broke to the plow. I will defend myself against the false accusations. God knows that I am innocent, and I intend to place my trust in Him."

"You do not know what they've all become," Tom cried. "The justices are bloodthirsty. And the people—I saw the looks in their eyes during the trial. They are no longer your friends, Aunt Odilia. They are a mob and will act as such!"

"Let them come," Odilia Prescott said, her dark eyes shining. "I am not afraid."

Tom fell back against a tree and buried his fingers in his long, wind-tossed, dark hair. "I cannot bear to have you maltreated as was Dorcas Manwell . . ." he whispered.

"But don't you see, child? If I run, I am perpetuating the existence of witches," Aunt Odilia explained. "Then they will look for others. Who knows how many innocent people will suffer? It is my duty to stand against them. Someday Tom Stockton, you, too, may be called to defend a great cause at the risk of your own life. And you must not run either. If good people do not stand against injustice, evil and darkness will triumph."

Tom sighed and said, "All right, Aunt, but be careful. Please, *be careful!*"

* * *

The following day, word reached the Stockton family that Odilia Prescott had been arrested for "sundry acts of witchcraft." But Dorcas Manwell was taking no chances with her freedom by accusing only one person. Also arrested was Ezekiel Fowler. The widow claimed the man had lifted a gun merely by putting four fingers into its barrel. The constable agreed that anyone with that much strength must indeed be a witch.

Tom went into town that day to pick up supplies. As he approached the dry goods store, he passed many people he knew. He tipped his hat to them, but most met his greeting with cold stares. Even Mr. Smythe, whose store Tom's family had been customers at for years, was distant in his dealings with Tom.

As Tom left the store, he met Martha Burnside and her family. Before Tom could speak, Mr. Burnside took his daughter's arm, saying, "Martha, we must be off."

Martha's mother seemed equally anxious that their daughter stay away from the nephew of an accused witch. But Martha whispered to Tom, "Meet me at two this afternoon at Laird's Crossing." Then she walked away with her parents.

That afternoon Tom went to Laird's Crossing, a small bridge that arched over a creek. Martha was about 10 minutes late. She hurried up and said breathlessly, "Mother thinks I'm making a dress with my cousin. Oh, Tom, I was so distressed when I heard the news of your aunt."

"Yes, I don't know what's gotten into the people of Northboro," Tom said.

"Please don't take this wrong," Martha said. "But have you ever witnessed behavior from your aunt that would support the accusations against her?"

Martha's question annoyed Tom. "Martha, Aunt Odilia is no more a witch than you are!" he said sharply. "She is a good, innocent woman. How could you think otherwise?"

Martha was silent a moment. Then she said, "Tom, you love her and that is commendable, but what if the charges be true?"

Tom cut her off in midsentence, "Those girls are liars, Martha. Have you not seen them going about Northboro, putting on shows so that people will pity them and give them gifts and favors?"

"Tom, unless you make it clear that you and your family reject your aunt and her works, you will put yourselves in danger," Martha said.

"My aunt's only works are works of charity," Tom said bitterly. "Are you saying that I should leave her alone in her hour of trial to save myself? Is that what you ask of me, Martha? To be a coward?"

Martha looked down at the grass around her feet. She swallowed hard and said in a faint voice, "My parents have forbidden me to see you again, Tom, unless you turn from Odilia Prescott. They say you must make it clear that she is no longer a member of your family."

9 Tom stared hard at Martha. She was the loveliest girl he had ever looked upon. Many times it had crossed his mind to marry her and make a life with her on the farm. Even though the wild seas and the distant horizon called to him, he considered giving it all up to spend his life with someone like Martha. But how could he marry a girl who allowed her thoughts to be swayed by three spoiled children? And how could he marry a girl who disapproved of one of his relatives? He knew he couldn't. That's all there was to it. And so he said, "Good-bye, Martha."

Martha's chin trembled, and her eyes filled with tears. "I did think that you felt love for me, Tom," she said.

"My heart is not able to love at such a price," Tom replied. "I will not betray my innocent kinswoman and my own conscience as well."

"Do I not mean more to you than your aunt?" Martha whispered.

Tom shook his head sadly and said, "I'm sorry, Martha. Good-bye." Then he turned and walked away.

When Tom returned home, Becky was waiting for him.

"Tom, I have an idea," Becky said. "We must go see Schoolmaster Hopkins."

"To what purpose?" Tom asked.

"We must ask him to come and testify against Aggie and her two friends," Becky said. "He saw on the scientific walk how those girls proved themselves to be frauds. If he will come to the meetinghouse and testify that the girls are lying, it could help Aunt Odilia."

"That is a worthy notion, little sister," Tom said smiling. He led the way to the wagon.

Schoolmaster Hopkins was a sour-tempered old man, who had lived in Northboro for over 30 years. But he was an excellent teacher and was devoted to imparting knowledge to his students. He was also well-respected by the townspeople.

But would he risk his own reputation to defend a woman accused of witchcraft? Tom wondered as the wagon bounced along. Would he have the courage?

When Tom and Becky reached the door

of the schoolteacher's house, they rapped. A moment later, Mr. Hopkins appeared. "What do you children want?" he asked bluntly.

"We are in a serious predicament, sir," Tom began. "You may have heard that our Aunt Odilia has been accused of witchcraft. We fear she will end up at the gallows unless we prove her innocent."

"I refuse to have anything to do with such affairs," Schoolmaster Hopkins declared. He started to close the door, but Becky spoke up.

"Please, sir," she said. "You're a wise and good man. Everyone in the village believes so. Surely you will not turn us away without listening."

The old man hesitated. Then he stepped back. "All right, come in and speak your piece," he said, "but do so quickly. I am a busy man."

He led them inside and showed them to the table in the kitchen. Tom and Becky took turns describing the situation. They explained to the old man how valuable his testimony against the girls might be.

Finally Schoolmaster Hopkins turned to

his wife, who had been cleaning nearby. "What think you, Hilda?"

Hilda Hopkins was as sour-tempered as her husband. Now she said decisively, "I think one ought to mind one's own business."

"Then you disapprove of my testifying on Odilia Prescott's behalf?" her husband asked.

"It is best not to meddle in so dangerous a subject as witchcraft," Mrs. Hopkins replied. "We are old, Amos. We have no need of such troubles."

Tom's heart sank. Schoolmaster Hopkins said, "I will consider your request. Go now, for I have things to do."

When Tom and Becky reached the wagon, Tom said, "I fear our cause is lost with the teacher. It appears as if his wife controls him."

"Maybe not," Becky said. "At school he tells stories of righteous people who dared all and oft times lost. Perhaps he will testify in spite of his wife."

"I hope you're right, Becky," Tom said.

Later at supper, Tom said, "I wish I

could visit Aunt Odilia. But she is allowed no visitors at the jail."

"It's a good thing," his father said. "It can do you no good to befriend her under the circumstances."

"I pray that when all this ends, we can get back to our normal lives," Tom's mother said.

Tom looked up sharply, "Does not the outcome matter to you, Mother?" he asked.

Mrs. Stockton looked sad. "Thomas, we can have no control over the outcome. The justices are wise men, experienced in the ways of witchcraft. We must accept their decision."

"I have oft warned my sister that her strange ways would one day cause her grief," Mr. Stockton said. "When Nehemiah was lost at sea, she should have remarried at once. There are many good men, widowers who yearn for a wife." He wrung his hands nervously. "It cannot bode well for this family if Odilia should be convicted. It is a mark upon us not easily erased. That is why we must not appear to be in league with her."

"Have you no love or concern for your sister, Father?" Tom asked angrily.

"Indeed, I wish this had not come to pass. But since it has, my first thought must be of my wife and children," his father answered. "Odilia chose her strange way of life. The best we can hope for is to be seen as a godly family, untainted by her sins."

Tom remembered his friend Peter's advice. *The only safe thing to do when family members are accused is to denounce them.* His parents were doing just that. They were disowning Aunt Odilia so that they would not be accused.

Once more a sense of helpless rage swept over Tom. He had to do something more. He could not stand idly by and watch his aunt be accused of so heinous a crime. It was then that Tom thought of Minister Waller. Few people in town knew of Odilia Prescott's many acts of charity. How she paid for burials of the poor. How she sent food to needy families. How she knitted mittens for the orphans of the village. Minister Waller knew though. He knew even better than Tom. Perhaps Tom could convince him to testify on Odilia's behalf.

Early the next day, Tom rode to Pembroke Village to see Minister Waller. The minister welcomed Tom warmly, obviously glad to see an old acquaintance. But when Tom told the minister the purpose of his visit, the man's face clouded.

"I very much fear I will myself be accused," he said. "When I tried to speak on behalf of Dorcas Manwell, they attacked me and even drove me from Northboro. What would they think if I appealed for another accused of witchcraft?"

"I asked Schoolmaster Hopkins to testify that he witnessed the duplicity of the three girls. But his wife bade him be silent. I am afraid her word will prevail. I am desperate, Minister Waller. I know you could testify to Aunt Odilia's many acts of charity," Tom said.

"Indeed, she is one of the most generous people in Northboro," Minister Waller admitted. "She is a good soul and surely innocent. I have no doubt of it."

"If you could come to Northboro and

tell that to the justices, I know it would help," Tom said. "You are my last hope."

Minister Waller wrung his hands. "Tom, do you not know that I have a wife and two young children?" he asked. "What will become of them if my testimony condemns me?"

Minister Waller's wife, Beth, came into the room just then. She held a baby in her arms while another child clung to her skirts. She was a quiet, kindly woman who had helped her husband serve the people of Northboro while they were there. Most of the townspeople liked her for her good heart and her refusal to gossip.

Tom felt sorry for Minister Waller. He did have to think of his family. How could Tom expect him to put them at risk? And yet, Tom *had* to plead because it was Aunt Odilia's only chance if Schoolmaster Hopkins did not come.

"Minister Waller, Odilia Prescott may go to the gallows if none has the courage to make known her good deeds," Tom said.

The minister's wife spoke up then. "She was the only one who would go to the Keyes family when they were stricken with a contagious disease," she said. "Do you remember, Charles?"

"I well remember," Minister Waller replied.

"And have you so soon forgotten your last sermon?" Mrs. Waller went on. " 'If God is on our side, we have nothing to fear from the works of men' you said. Do you not believe that yourself?"

Minister Waller looked at his young wife. "It is not for myself that I tremble. It is for the fate that would befall you and the babes should I be accused along with Odilia Prescott," he said. He turned to Tom then and said, "We will pray to God that truth will triumph, but it is all we can do. Do not ask us for more."

Beth Waller accompanied Tom out to his wagon. As he turned to climb aboard, she grasped his hand and said, "Have faith, Tom. All may not be lost."

10 Tom rode sadly back to Northboro. He doubted that Minister Waller's wife could convince her husband to testify. He wondered what he would do if he were in the places of Minister Waller and Schoolmaster Hopkins. Would he risk his life? Would he put his family in danger for Odilia Prescott? An odd woman who lived in a weather-grayed old house with only a few chickens and three pigs for company?

Three days later, the justices were again assembled in the meetinghouse. Odilia was brought in with her hands and feet in chains just as Dorcas Manwell had been. Unlike the widow, though, Odilia Prescott was not shamefaced and broken in spirit. Her shoulders were thrust back, and she sat ramrod straight. When Tom met her gaze, a defiant smile flickered on her lips. Her jaw was set in a kind of determination that Tom recognized from her way of living. She had more courage than most people Tom knew.

"Do not look upon her," Mr. Stockton cautioned.

"It is already done, Father," Tom replied. "I have smiled at her to bolster her courage."

Also brought in was Ezekiel Fowler, the man Dorcas Manwell had accused. Fowler was the first to be questioned.

"Ezekiel Fowler," Mr. Landis asked, "do you admit to being able to hoist a gun using only four fingers?"

"Well . . . yes," Mr. Fowler said hesitantly. "It is an old trick I learned as a young man."

"Then you admit to having superhuman strength?" Mr. Landis asked.

"No, no, not at all," Mr. Fowler protested. "It is merely a feat of balance I—"

But Mr. Landis cut him off. "Ezekiel Fowler, why do you hurt these children?" he demanded.

"I hurt no one," Mr. Fowler replied.

"Why do you commit sundry acts of witchcraft against these children?" Mr. Landis pressed.

Fowler lowered his eyes and bit his lip nervously, obviously at a loss as to what to say. Immediately Agatha Palmer cried, "Look! He bites his lip, and so I am bitten and I bleed. Oh, it hurts so much."

Fowler looked up, shocked. "But no, I

have done nothing!" he protested. "I am only a poor laborer, who never dealt harm to man or beast. Why do you do this to me?"

Suddenly Miriam Dow pointed above Ezekiel's head and shouted, "Look, he is rising to the ceiling!"

No one else in the room saw Ezekiel Fowler rising to the ceiling from his chair. But many people cowered, thinking he would pounce on their heads.

"Oh, he bit me too!" Belinda squealed. To the shock of the spectators, blood appeared on her lip.

By now the room was in chaos. Some screamed accusations at Ezekiel Fowler. Others rose from their chairs, ready to seize the accused.

"Silence!" one of the justices shouted. "Silence, I say!"

Finally the justice ordered that Ezekiel Fowler and Odilia Prescott be removed from the room. He allowed the children to be taken outside to recover from the ordeal. There, the parents washed the girls' faces and consoled them. A few minutes later, the girls returned. They walked cheerfully around the room and chatted with their friends and neighbors. They acted like celebrities, basking in the midst of the attention they received.

But as Agatha walked by Tom, he leaned forward and whispered, "Woe to you on judgment day when you are called to answer to the Almighty for your lies. He knows what is in your heart. Your miserable little performance will carry no weight on that awful day of judgment."

Agatha looked at Tom with fear in her eyes. He could see that for a moment she was truly frightened of the consequences of her actions. She opened her mouth as if to speak to him but then stopped. Her eyes narrowed then, and the look of fear was replaced by one of hatred.

Suddenly Agatha cried out, "Thomas Stockton is trying to choke me!" She threw herself to the floor and rolled back and forth.

Tom looked around in panic. He expected the constable to grab him at any moment and force him to the front of the room. But just as Agatha started her act, the accused were led back into the room.

And people began shouting accusations at them again. Amidst all the noise, Agatha's accusations were lost.

Tom watched as Aunt Odilia was led to the stand. The crowd quieted when Mr. Landis approached her.

"Odilia Prescott," Mr. Landis said, "do you understand the charges of witchcraft that have been brought against you?"

"I am innocent of all charges," Odilia Prescott declared.

"You do not admit then to sundry acts of witchcraft against these children?" Mr. Landis asked.

"God knows I am innocent," Odilia replied. "You may be able to fool yourselves with this nonsense, but you do not fool God. And you do not frighten me."

"The witch is unrepentant," Agatha Palmer's father shouted.

Agatha promptly leaped into the air and came crashing down on her chair, screaming, "She is looking at me! She is looking at me! Turn her around, make her stop!"

Miriam and Belinda were about to join

in when the door to the meetinghouse opened. With his head held high, Minister Waller walked into the room.

Tom's heart leaped with joy. So the young minister had overcome his fears and come after all! Beth Waller had been more persuasive than Tom had expected.

"Honorable justices," Minister Waller said, "allow me to speak. I have testimony as to the character of one of the accused."

"Speak you, sir," one of the justices said.

Minister Waller looked out over the packed meetinghouse. "I wish to say that Odilia Prescott has a long history of giving alms to the poor and needy," he said. "I have here the ledger books I kept while in the service of the church. Upon examination, you will see that few in Northboro were more generous than Odilia Prescott."

He handed the ledgers to one of the justices, who began to examine them. After a few minutes, the justice looked up and said, "This indeed speaks well for the accused. But is it not possible, Minister, that these charitable acts were done to quiet your suspicions concerning Odilia Prescott's darker activities?"

"I had no cause for such suspicions, sir," Minister Waller replied. "Odilia Prescott gave from the heart because she wanted to and for no other reason."

A few of the people looked moved by the revelation of Odilia's generosity. But most faces remained hardened. Upon seeing that the resolve of some of the audience was weakening, the girls doubled their efforts. Agatha became totally rigid, her arms and legs thrust out. She clenched her teeth and then seemed to gasp for breath. Miriam moaned and thrashed around wildly. Before long she cut her chin on a table leg, causing blood to course dramatically down her neck. Belinda cried out that Odilia Prescott was flying around the room.

And then the door opened again. And a tall, stooped figure entered, causing the clamor to subside.

"It is Schoolmaster Hopkins," several people whispered respectfully.

Nearly everyone in the room had been instructed by Amos Hopkins. No one doubted his wisdom or integrity. When he walked into a room, he was treated with respect by all.

Now the schoolmaster looked at the afflicted children and commanded, "These girls are my students. I refuse to allow their suffering to continue a moment longer. Remove the accused at once, and restore the children to tranquility."

"Yes!" arose an angry chorus of agreement. "Remove the witches!"

"Pity the children," a woman cried. "Schoolmaster Hopkins has spoken wisely as usual."

Once more, Odilia Prescott and Ezekiel Fowler were taken out. Immediately the girls became peaceful and smiling.

"Thank you, Teacher," Agatha said sweetly.

Tom stared at the proceedings, stunned by the teacher's behavior. Tom had begged him to come to rescue Aunt Odilia. But instead he was siding with the three girls and sealing the fate of the accused!

Schoolmaster Hopkins now turned to Agatha Palmer. "Dear child, are you quite composed now?"

"Oh yes, Teacher. I am well as long as the witches are locked away where they cannot look on me," Agatha replied.

All eyes in the room turned toward the tender scene. The tall, white-haired old gentleman speaking gently with the afflicted girl. Calming her fears, sympathizing with her.

Then suddenly, in a voice like a thunderbolt, Schoolmaster Hopkins cried out, "Alas! The witches have *not* gone! They are in the next room, peeking out at us from behind the door!" He pointed at the door through which the accused had been led.

Once more, Agatha Palmer fell to the floor and rolled about as if in agony. "My throat!" she cried. "I feel the burning!"

Miriam Dow gasped and coughed. "Oh yes, I feel it too!" she moaned.

"Make it stop! Make it stop!" Belinda sobbed. "Take them away. Oh, take them away. They torture us so!"

Schoolmaster Hopkins walked to the adjoining room and flung open the door, revealing the room to be empty. He demanded of the constable the whereabouts of the witches.

"They are back in prison, sir," the constable replied. "The wagon took them away a few minutes ago."

The tall old man turned, and his gaze swept the packed room. He stared first at the girls, then at the justices in their solemn black robes.

"Take note and listen," Schoolmaster Hopkins said. "When the girls were told that the witches were near, they immediately went into their act. But there were no witches behind that door. So the performance was a fraud. Witchcraft did not make these three girls gasp and cough and tumble about. They caused their own convulsions. The devil is indeed at work in Northboro. But the devil works not through witches but through the bitter lies of attention-seeking children!"

The justices stared down at Agatha Palmer. "Agatha Palmer, what say you to this charge?" asked one justice.

"The witch . . . Odilia Prescott . . . she cast her evil eye . . ." Agatha stammered. "She was choking me . . ."

"Odilia Prescott is far from here in the village jail," the justice said.

"There must be another . . . there must be another," Agatha said, looking around desperately. Tears ran down her cheeks, and her voice faltered. Miriam and Belinda, stunned by the developments, clung to each other in silence.

Agatha's desperate gaze finally fell upon Tom. "It is he—Tom Stockton—who did it! Oh, I suffer so!" she cried, clutching at her throat.

But instead of the usual clamor that accompanied the girls' antics, the room was silent. No one bothered to look at Tom. All eyes were upon Agatha Palmer. But no eyes held sympathy for her this time. Not even her parents'.

Agatha turned and ran to her mother, burying her face in her shoulder. "Oh, Mother! I suffer so. I suffer so," she sobbed.

Mr. Palmer took firm hold of the girl's arm and pulled her away from her mother. "Not so much as you shall, Agatha Palmer. Wait until we get you home. Then you will know the true meaning of suffering!"

"Free the accused!" declared the justice. "This trial is adjourned!"

The crowd filed out of the

meetinghouse then. Tom followed Schoolmaster Hopkins to his wagon.

"Thank you, Schoolmaster," Tom said. "I shall never forget what you did for my aunt."

The old man smiled. "It was my finest hour, Tom. The first opportunity I have ever had to risk my life for a noble cause. I grasped it, for I may never be called upon again. For years, I've told the children of Northboro about courage. Now I was given the chance to display it. Thank *you*, Tom Stockton."

Tom remembered the words of Aunt Odilia then. *If good people do not stand against injustice, evil and darkness will triumph.* Smiling, he headed for the jailhouse to take his aunt home.

* * *

Witch hunt hysteria spread through the state of Massachusetts for the next 30 years. Probably the most infamous—and deadly—of the trials that resulted were the Salem witch trials. From June through September of 1692, hundreds of people from the small village faced accusations of witchcraft. Dozens waited in jail for months without trials. And 19 were hanged on Gallows Hill.

But Thomas Stockton was long gone from Massachusetts by that time. In 1664, when he was 20, Tom left Northboro and went to Boston. That same year he sailed to the West Indies, the first of many voyages he took to strange and faraway places. At the age of 30, Tom was able to buy his own ship. He used the money he received from the sale of Odilia Prescott's farm. His beloved aunt had died earlier that year of pneumonia. Tom christened his new ship *The Odilia.* And as his aunt would have wanted, he spent the rest of his life on the seas.

Novels by Anne Schraff

PASSAGES

An Alien Spring
Bridge to the Moon (Sequel to *Maitland's Kid*)
The Darkest Secret
Don't Blame the Children
The Ghost Boy
The Haunting of Hawthorne
Maitland's Kid
Please Don't Ask Me to Love You
The Power of the Rose (Sequel to *The
    Haunting of Hawthorne*)
The Shadow Man
The Shining Mark (Sequel to *When a Hero Dies*)
A Song to Sing
Sparrow's Treasure
Summer of Shame (Sequel to *An Alien Spring*)
To Slay the Dragon (Sequel to *Don't Blame
    the Children*)
The Vandal
When a Hero Dies

PASSAGES 2000

The Boy from Planet Nowhere
Gingerbread Heart
The Hyena Laughs at Night
Just Another Name for Lonely (Sequel to
    Please Don't Ask Me to Love You)
Memories Are Forever

PASSAGES to History

Dear Mr. Kilmer
Dream Mountain
Hear That Whistle Blow
Strawberry Autumn
Winter at Wolf Crossing